How the Bear Met the Bee

By Ashley Sollenberger

Pictures by Amber Kane

When a bear and bee meet,

It might be a battle for that bee's tasty treat.

But a few weeks ago –
On a fine sunny day...
The bear met a bee
In a most unusual way!

The bear looked around and yawned a **big** yawn.

That yawn made a breeze
ever so slight.

The bee left the hive and took
her first **flight**.

She got caught on that breeze blowing so slight.

That little breeze **blew** her off to the right.

And into a bus ...
now that was a **sight.**

The driver went bonkers with the bee on the bus, he honked on the **horn** and made a big fuss.

The brown bear heard the **horn**, which was not the norm.

He started to **run** as
if chased by a storm.

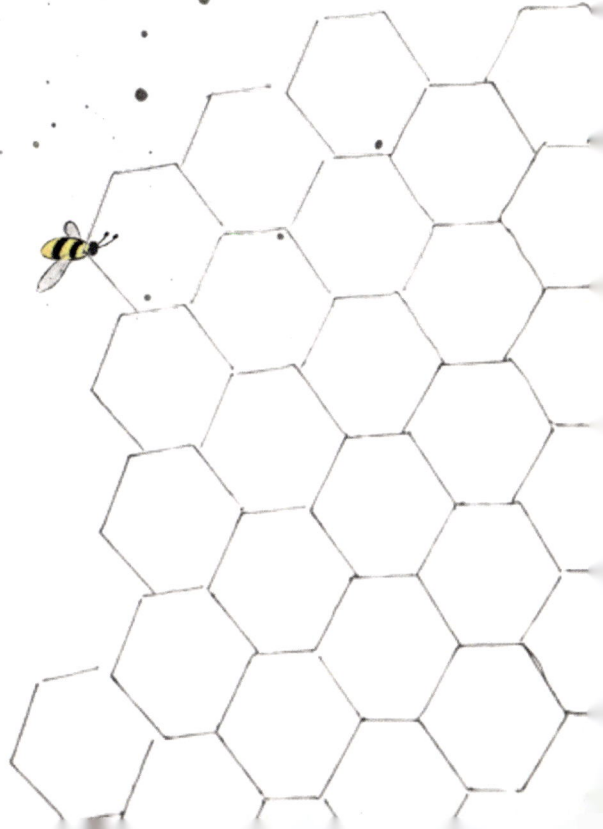

The boys and girls
playing baseball all
stopped to yield, for all
of a sudden a bear was
out on the field.

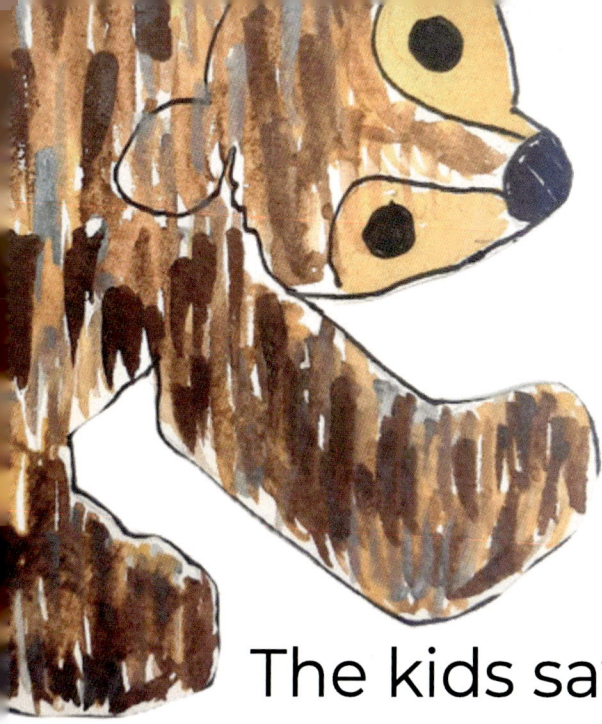

The kids saw the bear so they ran toward the bus.

Where they tried to get on in a crazy fast rush.

The kids on the bus heard the driver whisper......

HUSH!

Then the driver pointed and said really slow...

There's a bee...

On my knee!

The kids in a panic now started to **flee**.
What did their little eyes see?

One poor boy named Chase was standing just off the base.

The **bear** was still **running,** but it was no **race**.

That bear **tagged** the boy out at home base.

The kids lost in a rout now that Chase was tagged out!

The kids with a **frown** all put their heads down.
The bee saw her chance and **flew** out the door.
She did not want to be on that bus anymore.

The bee now in flight,
flew towards a flower. She needed to eat.
It had been a crazy last hour.

The bear was still running away from the team, he was heading right toward a nice freshwater stream.

On the edge of that stream grew something **sweet.** The bee would finally get something to eat.

She **flew** down to the flower from such a great height.
But under the water a fish hid out of sight.

The fish **jumped** to catch the bee still in flight. When all of a sudden, the bear took **a bite.**

The bear caught the fish.
The bee was alright.

And that my dear friend is **how the bear met the bee** in sunny daylight.

Ashley is a father and elementary PE teacher. He incorporates imagination and movement into his teaching. He often ties together bits of real life from his childhood and teaching experiences into his writing.

Amber is a creative thinker, dreamer, educator, and curriculum developer. Her love for art and experience in ed tech, made her the perfect partner to help bring Ashley's idea to reality.

Ashley and Amber are siblings and this is their first work together. Ashley previously wrote and published "How the Tree Became Happy."

Related activities

Visit: **https://bit.ly/bearandbee** to download activities pages and discover additional resources.

Bus

__ __ __

Bee

___ ___ ___

Bear

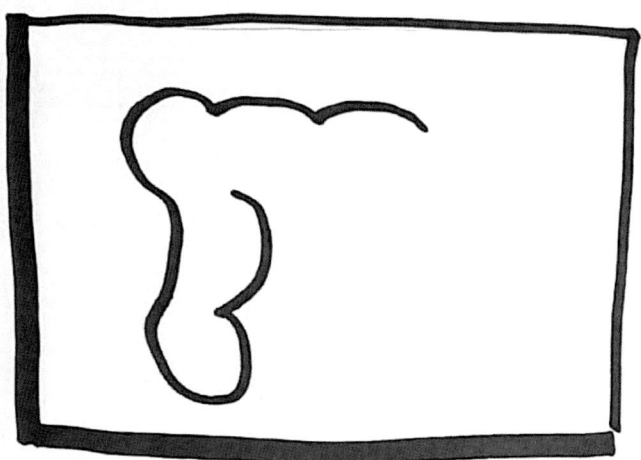

Activity #1

Practice: Write the letters on the lines provided to spell words.

Identify: Circle two words that best describe how the person or animal moves.

Bee

_____ _____ _____

How does a bee move?
Circle two choices.

Fast

Slow

Zig-zag

Straight

Bear

_____ _____ _____ _____

How does a bear move?
Circle two choices.

Roaming

Slow

Jumping

Gallop

Baseball Players

Boy

_____ _____ _____

Girl

_____ _____ _____ _____

How does a baseball player move?

Circle two choices.

Fast

Skip

Slow

Straight

Activity #2

Practice
Move to a large room or outside.
Select a leader (student or teacher)
Demonstrate movement: The leader states what animal or person they are pretending to be, and demonstrates a connected movement.
Mirror: Students, listen to and watch the leader, then mirror the movement through practice.

Play
The leader will call out, bee, baseball player, or bear. Students will listen, remember, and move based on the word.

Combinations
Change locomotor skills and have students "skip like a bee".
Example:
Bee= students make a high curvy movement.
Bear= students move slowly, and roam in a curving path.

Additional Objects
Select additional objects and demonstrate movement and practice.

Make it a Game

Play tag or a version of red light, green light using the objects and movements to guide how students move during the game.

Example: green light, baseball , students would move fast like a ball, or roll on the ground.

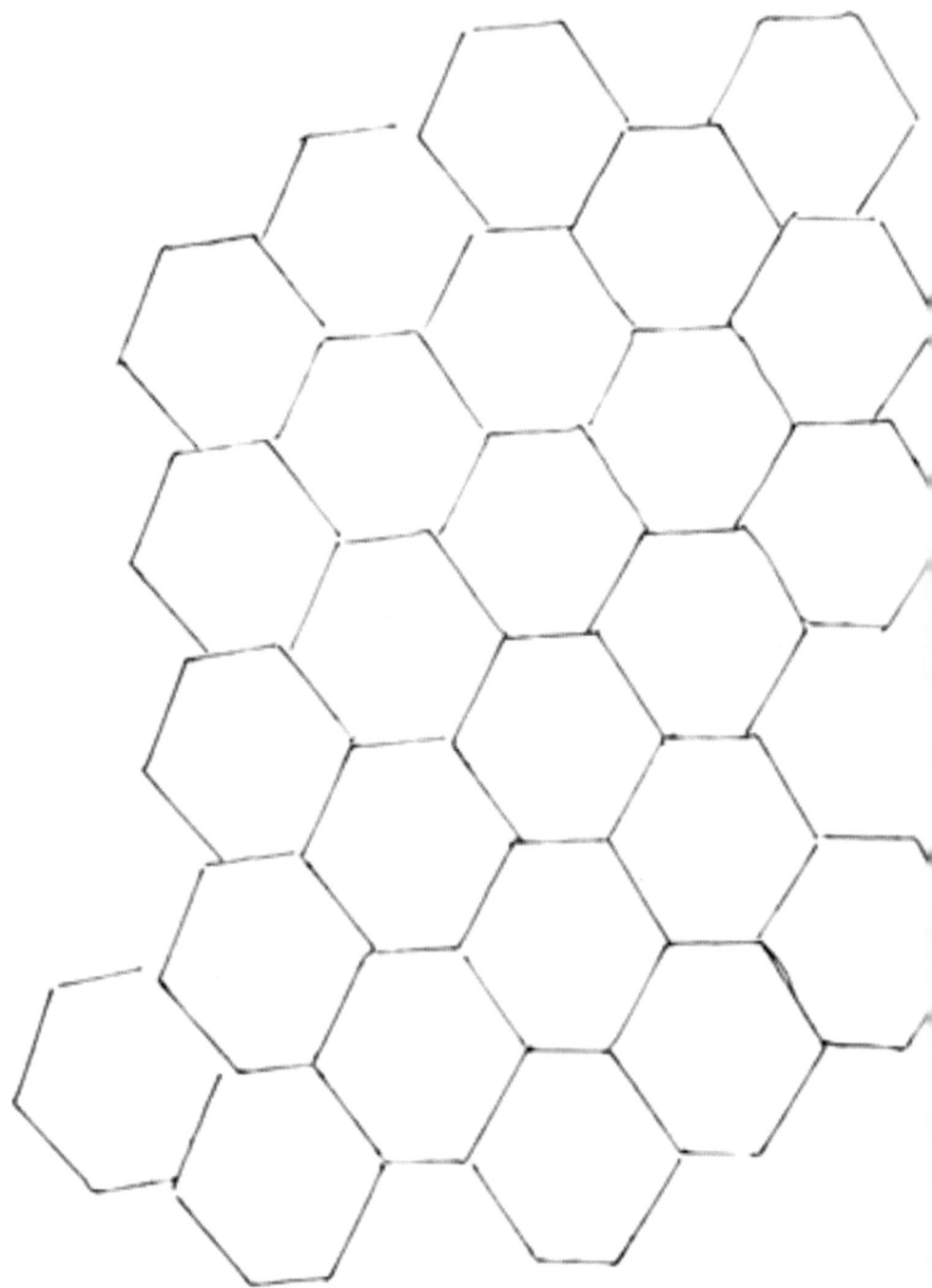

Made in the USA
Middletown, DE
09 November 2021